Being the "new kid" was NOT cool.

I'd never been so happy to see another dog in my whole life. He was about the same size as me, only kind of fat.

"Hi," I wagged.

"What are you doing in MY yard?" he growled.

"Huh . . . who, me?" I stammered. "I . . . er . . ."

"This is MY yard. GET OUT!"

I wagged my tail and took another step toward him. "No, wait. You don't understand . . ."

"You don't get out, I'll bite your head off."

"But . . . but . . ."

Short, stubby legs popped like springs. The dog took one little hop. I saw the white as his teeth flashed. Before I could jerk back . . .

HE BIT ME—right on the very tip of my nose!

Books by Bill Wallace

Red Dog
Trapped in Death Cave

Available from ARCHWAY Paperbacks

The Backward Bird Dog
Beauty
The Biggest Klutz in Fifth Grade
Blackwater Swamp
Buffalo Gal
The Christmas Spurs
Danger in Quicksand Swamp
Danger on Panther Peak
(Original title: Shadow on the Snow)
A Dog Called Kitty
Ferret in the Bedroom, Lizards in the Fridge
The Final Freedom
Journey into Terror
Never Say Quit
Snot Stew
Totally Disgusting!
True Friends
Watchdog and the Coyotes

Available from MINSTREL Books

BILL WALLACE

The BACKWARD BIRD DOG

Illustrated by David Slonim

A MINSTREL® BOOK

Published by POCKET BOOKS
New York   London   Toronto   Sydney   Tokyo   Singapore

A MINSTREL PAPERBACK *Original*

 A Minstrel Book published by
POCKET BOOKS, a division of Simon & Schuster Inc.
1230 Avenue of the Americas, New York, NY 10020

ISBN: 0-671-56852-3

First Minstrel Books printing August 1997

10 9 8 7 6 5 4 3 2 1

A MINSTREL BOOK and colophon are registered trademarks of
Simon & Schuster Inc.

Cover art by David Slonim

Printed in the U.S.A.

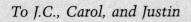

To J.C., Carol, and Justin

Chapter 1

Old Blue howled at night.

It was a mournful sound. Soft and low, it crept through the darkness of our kennel that warm summer evening like a snake. The sadness of its cold hard coils wrapped around me, cutting off all the love and comfort that was so near.

I pressed my ears flat against my head, trying to shut out his cry. Still it got through. It made my insides feel as cold and lonely as he was. It hurt.

I shivered and raised my head. Mother was right beside me. I pushed closer to her, hoping her warmth would chase away the chills and the scaries.

"Why does Old Blue cry like that?" I asked.

"He's sad," she answered.

1

"Why is he sad?"

"He has no nose and he has no My."

I cocked an ear and tilted my head to the side. "What happened to his nose? Did he get it bit off in a fight?"

Mother's tail thumped against the floor. "He really does have a nose," she laughed. "Only it doesn't work. He can't smell quail with it."

"Quail?"

"Yes," she answered. "You see, we're bird dogs. We find quail for our Mys. When we find them, we point at them so our Mys can shoot them. That makes them happy and proud. Old Blue has a nose, but he can't find quail. A bird dog must have a good nose to make our My happy."

"What's a My?"

"A My is a People. Not just any People," she explained. "It's a very special People you love and who loves you."

"What's love?"

Mother took a deep breath. I could feel her sides heave in and out against my cheek. "Love is sort of a thing. Well, no . . . it's more of a feeling . . . it's . . . it's . . . well, love is really hard to explain."

"Please try, Mother," I urged with a shove of my nose. "Please. I really want to know."

Her ears flopped when she shook her head. "I can't. But when you love or when someone loves you . . . well, you just know."

"Will I have a My?"

"Someday."

"And I'll just know, right?"

"You'll know. Now go to sleep before you wake your brothers and sisters."

I lay my head on my paws and closed my eyes. Old Blue howled again. My eye popped open. I crawled over Mother's paw and scooted right up against her cheek. I got so close that my eyeball almost touched hers.

"If I have a nose that doesn't work . . . if I don't have a My . . . will I howl at night, like Old Blue? Will I make his sad, scary sound?"

The big brown eye that stared at me blinked. Mother glanced away for just an instant, then the big brown eye smiled down at me.

"You're such a worrywart."

"What's a worrywart?"

"A puppy who asks dumb questions and keeps his mother awake all night." She winked. "Now, hush and go to sleep. You're going to be just fine."

With that, Mother began to kiss me. Her tongue wrapped about me like a warm blanket. It chased away the scary sadness of Old Blue's howl. It made me feel safe.

If Mother said I was going to be just fine . . . well, that was good enough for me. That's because mothers are about the wisest and bestest

3

things in the whole entire world. Safe and warm, I closed my eyes.

Early the next morning, Roberto and Mr. Tommy opened the top of our bedroom. Mr. Tommy lifted Mother out and closed the roof. My brothers and sisters and I waddled through the opening into the wire pen. Our pen was high up off the ground. But even though our feet slipped through the wire floor all the time, we didn't worry about falling. That was because the openings in the wire were too small for us to fall all the way to the ground. We watched Mother run all around the big yard. She sniffed here and there and used the bathroom, then sniffed some more places. Finally, Mr. Tommy called to her and she came back. Roberto lifted her into the wooden part of our pen and closed the roof. We all scrambled inside with Mama to lie on the hay and get breakfast.

We'd just finished eating when this machine monster came into the Big Yard and stopped by the People house. A man People and a woman People got out. Mr. Tommy went to greet them and they spent a long time making mouth noises. Then the Peoples followed Mr. Tommy all around our kennel. They looked at each dog and made mouth noises. All the dogs wagged their tails and barked and spun around and jumped with their front paws on the chain-link fence.

When they came to Old Blue's pen, he just lay there and looked at them.

The man People and Mr. Tommy spent a long time in front of Big Mike's pen. But it wasn't long before the woman People came over to where we were. My brothers and sisters and I always got excited when a People came by to look at us. Nobody really understood why. I mean, they *are* kind of ugly creatures. Still, there's just something about them that made us all wiggly inside.

Tina was the first to greet her. Tina always was better about walking on the wire than the rest of us. She wagged her tail and stuck her nose through the pen. The woman People rubbed her, then reached in to scratch behind Tina's ears. By then, Ben was there. He shoved Tina out of the way so he could get touched by the woman People, too. I was hot on Ben's heels, but my paw slipped through one of the holes in the wire and I fell. I bumped my chin so hard that it crossed my eyes. It didn't take me long to get up, but it was long enough that Pat and the rest of my brothers and sisters raced past me and got to the edge of the pen first.

The woman People had a soft, pretty voice. She laughed and smiled and petted each of my brothers and sisters. I shoved Pat out of the way with my nose and shoulder. She didn't pet me, though. Instead, she bent way down and looked me square in the eye.

5

"Bill." She made a mouth noise that was so loud it made me blink. "Come over here and look at this little fella."

I took a step back and my hind foot fell through the wire. Ben shoved in front of me. The woman People didn't pet him. She didn't even look at him. Her eyes were still on me.

"See you found the puppies," Mr. Tommy said.

The woman People didn't mouth talk to him. Instead, she kept looking at me. She leaned a bit to the side so the man People could stand next to her.

"Looks a lot like old Slim, doesn't he?" Her voice was very soft, almost sad.

The man People frowned at me. Then he smiled like the woman People did.

"Sure does."

"He's got blue eyes." She reached to pet me as I wedged my way between Ben and Sassy. "Never saw a dog with blue eyes."

"I never noticed that," Mr. Tommy admitted. "He sure does. They'll change, though. As he gets older, they'll turn to what we call deer eyes—sort of a soft brown. It is kind of unusual, though."

I couldn't quite understand all their People noises, but I could tell they were talking about me. I could tell by the way all their eyes were on me. The woman People reached past my brothers and sisters to pet me. Even when Sassy and Pat tried to knock me out of the way, she ignored them

6

and scratched behind my ears. I liked the way she touched and rubbed.

They made more mouth noises, then started to walk away.

"Hey, don't leave," we all yelled. "This is fun. Come on back."

They didn't listen. Despite all our wiggling and wagging and scents, they walked to look in the other pens.

But when they were just a few feet away, the woman People stopped and turned. Even with all my brothers and sisters clamoring all over one another and jumping this way and that, and even with Tiny and me on the bottom, she looked straight at me.

There was something special about that look. Something that made an excited, yet warm and easy feeling come inside. I liked her. I liked her a bunch.

After a while, they got back in their machine monster and left. The woman People looked at me one last time. I got that same warm feeling from her look, but when they left, the feeling went with them. At the time, I didn't think anymore about it.

Besides, I could always ask Mother. She would know why the woman People's look made me feel the way I did. Mother would tell me. Mother told us everything—except "leaving."

Chapter 2

I guess there are a lot of things to learn when you're little. Mother was about the best place to go to find out stuff. Of course, there were a lot of things we had known—right from the very beginning. These were things Mother didn't have to teach us because our inside feelings had already told us.

Inside, we knew stuff like—birds were the most interesting thing in the world, next to People. We'd never seen a snake, but our inside feelings told us that we didn't need to mess with them and it was best to leave the nasty things alone. Our inside feelings told us how to move our feet in deep water, although the deepest water was in the drinking bowl next to Mother's food. It only came up to our ankles.

Mother had told us to trust our feelings. Mostly she taught about People animals.

One of the most important things she had told us was that they couldn't understand Dog. No matter how much we blinked, wiggled our ears, held our tail this way and that, or gave our smells—People animals just didn't get it.

"We learn about the world with our nose," she had explained. "Our nose is the most important thing we have and we need to take good care of our nose. But when People animals learned to make mouth noises . . . well, they lost their nose. They can't talk to each other with smells. The only way they can communicate is with mouth noises."

"Do People animals howl at night like Old Blue?" I asked.

Mother frowned at me and twitched an ear. "Huh?"

"You said they lost their nose," I answered with a wiggle of my whiskers. "You told me that Old Blue lost his nose. So do people howl at night like Old Blue does?"

Mother smiled. "No. They depend on us and our nose to find quail for them."

"What are quail?" Tiny wondered.

"We are bird dogs and quail are birds," Mother answered. "But not just any bird. They have the most wonderfully delicious smell in the whole world. In fact, it's the second best smell there is."

"What's the best smell?" I asked.
"Proud."
"What's Proud?"
Mother's chest puffed really big. "It's a smell that our Mys give when they love us so much they can hardly stand it. When we find quail and point them, it makes our Mys proud. And Proud is the best smell ever!"

Mother licked us with her tongue. She fed us her delicious milk and kept us warm. Having her close always seemed to chase away the angry voices that came from the other pens or from inside the barn. Her tongue on our faces and backs covered us like a blanket and protected us from the threatening smells and frightening sounds. Curled up next to her with my brothers and sisters made me safe from all the scary things of the night.

Then, when we were two months old, Mr. Tommy had taken us away from Mother.
He and Roberto just up and snatched all six of us right out of our pen. They put us in a new place. It had dirt for a floor instead of the thick heavy wire we were used to. I liked it better because my feet didn't fall through the holes when I tried to walk around. Of course, there was always poop to step in, but if you were careful . . .

Anyway, I liked the dirt floor. I liked the room, too. The pen was big and we could run and chase and play until we were ready to drop.

When night came, I didn't like it. My brothers and sisters didn't either. That was because Mother wasn't there. We whined and cried and barked almost all night, but she never came. Mother loved us. We just couldn't understand why she didn't come. She'd told us that Mr. Tommy was a nice People. But if he really was nice, why would he do something so mean as making us leave Mother? It just didn't make sense. I was lonely and sad, and even with my brothers and sisters around I was a little scared, too. Worst of all, Old Blue howled at night. My mother wasn't there to chase the sad and mournful sound from my ears and from my heart.

The next day, we played and chased and wrestled. It seemed to keep our minds off of how much we missed Mother. At night, nothing helped. The next day, we played even harder— maybe tonight we'd be so tired we wouldn't have to think about Mother.

A few days went by and this big machine monster rumbled and puttered into the Big Yard. A man People got out. Mr. Tommy came and both made the People noises with their mouths. They touched their paws together and pumped their arms up and down. Then Mr. Tommy went to the barn. We had been so excited when he brought Mother out, we could hardly stand it. It was wonderful to see her again! We jumped and leaped and barked and pounced and tumbled all over each other. Chuck even fell in some poop once. But we were so happy to see Mother that nobody so much as noticed.

We got even more excited when they came to look in our pen. While Mr. Tommy and the man People made mouth noises, we told Mother how happy we were to see her and how glad we were that she was coming back to us.

"But I'm not coming back," she said with a soft smile and a twist of her tail. "You're my babies and I'll always love you. But you're growing up. I can't stay with you forever. I have to go back home with My Gary."

"Oh, please, please! Don't leave us, Mother," we all whined at once.

"Now hush that," she ordered with a squint of her eyes and a soft growl. "It's time to leave. I want to go with My Gary. I love him and he loves me. He is very proud of me. Your My People will come before too long, and you will understand."

Bobby plopped on his haunches.

"Why do you love your Gary more than us?" He whimpered. "Why are People animals so important?"

13

Mother's ears went up.

"No one knows," she answered as honestly as she could. "It has always been this way, for as long as anyone remembers. We must have People before our lives are complete.

"You are my babies." Her ears arched and she stood even taller and straighter than I had ever seen. "I am a great bird dog. Your father was a great bird dog. You will be the best bird dogs EVER. I just know it. You'll be fine."

Something about the scents she gave and the way she held herself . . . well, it made us all feel sort of big and brave. We stood straight, too. I felt my chest begin to fill . . . then suddenly, I remembered Old Blue. Inside my head, I could hear his howls from last night. The air whooshed out of my chest.

"But, Mother," I shuddered. "What if we mess up? What if something bad happens to our nose? What if we don't make our My proud? Will they stop loving us? Will they stop being our My?"

Mother didn't have time to answer. The man People tugged on her rope. She didn't pull back. She didn't even try to stay with us. With a smile and her tail waving back and forth in the air, she trotted happily behind him.

"My Gary's ready to take me home," she wagged. "I hope your life is as rich and happy as mine. Take care of your nose. Love you all. Good-bye."

We sat down and watched her hop into the tummy of a big machine monster. It roared and puttered, then it took our mother away. I wished she had time to answer my question. It was really important. It worried me—especially at night when Old Blue howled.

Chapter 3

I played with my brothers and sisters. We romped and wrestled. Beth pulled Tiny's tail and when Tiny turned to snap at her she'd run. They chased each other round and round the pen. Over the next few weeks, People came and looked at us. Ben left with a man People and his little boy. Chuck was taken by a man People, only he didn't want to go because he was afraid it really wasn't his My. Things were quiet for a few days, then more People came. Excited, we all wiggled and jumped and wagged our tails. I liked People. But none left me with the feeling that the woman People had.

Then one day, she came back.
The man People and a boy People came with

her. And when she looked at me, I knew what
Mother had meant when she'd told us about
our My.

How I knew or why . . . well . . . I just knew.

Mr. Tommy let me out of the pen. I ran
straight to her and wiggled and jumped around
and tried to kiss her with my tongue.

She sat on the grass with her long hind legs
crossed. She held me and stroked my back.

"Come on," I wiggled and jerked. "I want to
show you how fast I can run. You can run with
me. It's fun. Let's go. Let's run!"

She just held me tighter and laughed with her
soft voice. The man People handed Mr. Tommy
some pieces of green paper, and the next thing
I knew . . .

It was warm in the tummy of the big monster.
The machine that swallowed us roared and shook
and zoomed. It was scary. The boy People sat
beside me. He was a big boy People—almost a
man People, but not quite. He rubbed my back.
That felt good, but not good enough to chase
away the scaries or make the roar and rumble of
the machine monster stop.

I could see the tops of trees every now and
then. They spun past so quickly I could hardly
tell they were trees. There were clouds in the
sky. Like the trees, they moved too, only not as
fast. It seemed like everything was whizzing and

whooshing. Despite the warm feeling in the machine monster's tummy and the boy People's comforting hand on my back, I still trembled.

"We can stop now," I told them with a twitch of my ear and a jerk of my rear end.

Nobody said anything.

"You can let me out now," I suggested with one of my best smells. "I'm ready to go back and play with my brothers and sisters. Okay?"

Nothing.

Everything was whizzing and spinning. My tummy growled. I squeezed my eyes shut. Tried to think of nice things that would chase the scaries away.

It didn't work. My tummy rolled.

"I don't feel so good," I told them. "I think you should stop and let me out." I twitched and wiggled and belched. "This is serious!"

They didn't understand.

This was horrible. Terrible. I felt totally rotten. If they didn't let me out of this monster so I could get some fresh air, I was afraid . . .

I threw up.

I felt rotten! Now you've done it, I thought. Great start! How can you expect your My to love you if you throw up? Throwing up has to be the worst thing in the world—especially when you're trying to make your People like you.

My tummy rolled again.

18

Oh, no! My My is going to take me back, I thought. They're going to put me in the pen with Old Blue. Nobody will ever love me. I'm gonna end up howling at night. I'm going to . . .

I threw up again.

Suddenly, there was a whole lot of mouth noises and jumping around inside the machine monster.

"Puppy carsick, Mama?" The man People glanced back at me.

"Yeah," my My answered.

She leaned over the top of the big cloth bench at the front of the machine monster. Carefully, she pulled the towel from under me. She sort of wadded the bad stuff up inside and used a dry corner to wipe my face. Then the boy People who sat beside me picked me up gently and my My slipped a fresh towel underneath. When the boy People laid me back down, I felt a little better.

My My smiled down at me and patted my head. I closed my eyes. I didn't feel good. I cocked an ear and opened one eye. My My was still smiling and patting my head. Despite how horrible I felt, her look almost wagged my tail.

There was no doubt in my mind as I felt her look. She was my My, all right. I mean, if she could still love me after I threw up—she just had to be my My. I closed my eyes and plopped my head on the clean towel.

*   *   *

The machine monster finally shut up. When they opened the doors, the fresh air made me feel better. They got out and the boy People put me on the ground. I didn't know where I was, but I could tell I was a long long ways from home. Nothing smelled the same. Nothing looked the same. I staggered, trying to get my balance and hoping my tummy would quit rolling.

Suddenly, a strange odor caught my nose. I leaned forward sniffing at the smell.

This fuzzy gray thing appeared. He rubbed against the big black paw of the machine monster. Yellow eyes grew tight when he spotted me.

"Hi," I wagged.

He didn't wag back. I took a few steps in his direction.

All at once, the gray thing went POOF! I mean, it was like one second he was just standing there and the next second he was twice as big—like he was about to blow up or something.

It stopped me dead in my tracks. I couldn't believe my eyes.

"Hey, what happened? How did you do that?"

"Back off," the gray thing hissed. "You're a dog. I hate dogs!"

"I'm a puppy," I corrected.

"That's even worse," he sneered.

I cocked an ear and took another step. "How'd you get so big?"

The gray thing's eyes narrowed. He arched his

back and raised the paw that was closest to me. Long sharp claws sprang out.

"I mean it." His lip curled. "You come any closer, I'm gonna rip your nose off."

I leaned closer. "You're not a dog, are you? If you'll just let me get close enough for one good smell . . ."

Before I could even blink, his paw flashed out. Then the other paw—both whacked me on the tip of the nose. I jumped so hard that I tumbled backward over my own tail. I ended up on my back with my feet in the air. I had to struggle to get to my feet, and just about the time I stood up, the pain hit.

It was like my nose was on fire.

"Oooouch!" I squealed. "That hurt! You really did . . . you ripped my nose off."

The boy People swooped me up in his arms and kicked at the gray thing. He didn't really hit him with his foot, but it scared him away. He tucked his tail, raced around the side of the machine monster, and climbed a big tree beside the People house.

Whimpering and crying, I crossed my eyes and looked down at the tip of my nose. It really wasn't gone. But there were two deep scratch marks right on the tip of my snout. It hurt! A little blood began to leak from the marks. It made me cry.

The boy People patted my head and the man

eople and my My talked to me real sweet. They
arried me away from the machine monster and
he tree where the gray thing glared down and
wished his tail at me.

I heard a squeaking sound when they opened a
ate. The boy People put me on the ground inside
small yard. There was a chain-link fence on one
ide, a lot like the fence at our kennel. On two
ther sides were black poles that went up and
own to make another fence, and on the fourth
ide of the little yard was the People house made
f brick. The boy People and my My went inside.
he man People put a little white stick in his
nouth. He coughed when he stuck fire to the
nd of it and blew smoke out of his face. Then
e sat down in a chair and blew more smoke.

With one eye on the tree where the gray thing
ent, I'd just started to explore the little yard
when I heard the door open.

I glanced around and saw a dog. I'd never been
o happy to see another dog in my whole life. He
was about the same size as me, only kind of fat.
act was, he was so big around he waddled when
e walked toward me. He had short white hair
n his back, and fuzzy, kind of long hair on his
hest and tummy. It hung down like a skirt that
women People sometimes wear. His ears were
harp and pointy and long hair drooped from his
hin and jaws, kind of like Mr. Tommy's beard.

"Hi," I wagged. "Did you see what just hap-

23

pened? This big, gray, fuzzy thing—he tried t
rip my nose off. You should have been here.
mean, no reason at all, he just up and swatte
me and . . ."

"What are you doing in MY yard?" he growle‹

"Huh . . . who, me?" I stammered. "I . .
er . . ."

"This is MY yard. GET OUT!"

I wagged my tail and took another step towar
him. "No, wait. You don't understand. This bi
gray thing . . . out there . . . and he . . ."

"You don't get out, I'll bite your head off."

"But . . . but . . ."

Short, stubby legs popped like springs. The do
took one little hop. I saw the white as his teet
flashed. Before I could jerk back . . .

HE BIT ME—right on the very tip of my nose

Chapter 4

*B*eing the "new kid" was NOT cool.

The gray thing scratched my nose. The dog bit my nose. Even though the People yelled at him and the boy People swatted him on the bottom and chased him back in the house, my nose still hurt. The People didn't like me, either—I guess. They just played with me for a little while before they went back inside.

I crossed my eyes and looked down my snout. My poor nose was starting to swell. It throbbed and pounded like somebody was whacking it with a stick. I was all alone with nothing to do.

Despite my sore nose, I sniffed at the black fence around the little yard. There was plenty of room between the up and down poles, so I squeezed through and went to explore.

Another fence surrounded a big yard. The fence was made of chain link, just like our pens back home. Only this pen was ENORMOUS. None of the cages back at the kennel were nearly this big. The little yard was almost all concrete. Here there was grass everywhere. I liked grass. There were trees, too. I followed the fence to the big trees at the left corner of the yard. Not far from the trees was a wood thing with plants growing in it. I trotted over and sniffed at the pink flowers that stood at the top of the plants. They smelled sweet, but I was careful not to get my nose too close when I saw the thorns. My nose hurt bad enough as it was. If one of those thorns stuck me . . .

There was another tree at the right corner of the yard. But instead of having a brown trunk, this one was green from the very bottom clear to the very top. It didn't have leaves. It had sharp pointed green needles all over it. I started over to investigate.

Suddenly, I froze in my tracks. My ears perked so high, the loose floppy skin around my neck almost choked me. My eyes got as big around as Mother's food bowl.

Right in the middle of all that grass in the big yard was concrete. And right in the middle of all that concrete was the most HUMONGOUS drinking bowl I had ever seen.

I inched closer—one step at a time.

My toenails scraped the concrete. Still keeping my hind feet on the grass, I leaned forward and sniffed. The water smelled funny. Not clean, fresh water that was good for drinking, this stuff made my nose sting and twitch. It was deep, too. The water was really clear and I could see all the way to the bottom. A little bark slipped from my throat when I realized that there was enough water in this drinking bowl to swallow me, my brothers and sisters, and all the dogs at Mr. Tommy's kennel. I plopped on my haunches and looked at it.

Why would anybody need such an enormous drinking bowl? I wondered.

"BUZZZZZ!"

The sudden sound startled me. I sprang to my feet and spun around. A bug landed on one of the sweet-smelling pink flowers that stood in a row along the back fence. "Buzzz," he said with his fluttering wings.

I cocked an ear and tilted my head. The bug stuck his head down inside of one of the pink flowers.

"What you doing?" I asked.

"Buzzz."

"I'm a puppy. I just got here. But I want to go home 'cause nobody likes me."

He didn't answer. Instead, he just stuck his head deeper into the pink flower. I moved a step or two toward him. "This fuzzy gray thing scratched my nose, then the dog bit me. My nose really hurts."

"Buzzz." He fluttered his wings and moved to another flower. The bug was sort of a bright red color with black wings. I couldn't see his face because he had it stuck down into one of the flowers, but his back end was kind of long and pointy.

I moved closer.

"Do you want to be my friend?"

"Buzzz."

"I could really use a friend right now." I confessed with a sigh. My head tilted in the other direction as I took another step toward him. "What'ya doin' in that flower?"

"Buzzz." He ignored me and flew a little ways to another pink flower.

I remember Mother telling us that we couldn't understand bugs. Still, I was really lonely, and the way this guy was moving from flower to flower and working so hard, it really made me curious.

"Are you getting something to eat? Are you playing down in there?"

"Buzzz."

Both ears shrugged. I couldn't understand buzzz, but maybe if I got close enough to smell— to look down in that pink flower and see what he was doing with his head down in there . . .

I stepped up right beside the bush with the

pink flowers. I leaned forward, easy and careful so I wouldn't startle him. I got closer and closer and closer until my nose was almost touching his rump.

Suddenly, his head popped from the flower. Big, bubblelike eyes glared at me.

"BUZZZ!" His back end whipped around. This sharp, pointy thing stuck out like a tail and . . .

WHAM!

He jabbed the pointy thing right into the tip of my nose.

"Yipe, yipe, yipe!" I screamed and jumped back.

I blinked. I felt water leak out of my eyes and trickle down my cheeks. I shook my head.

When the gray thing scratched me, it hurt. When the dog bit me, that really hurt. But this . . .

"Yipe, yipe, yipe," I cried again.

It just kept right on hurting. My nose got hotter and hotter and I couldn't stand it. I shook my head until my ears flopped. I backed up, but it didn't help. Frantically, I rubbed my nose with my paw. It didn't help, either. It just hurt more and more.

"Yipe!" I screamed. I had to get away from the hurt. I couldn't stand it. I wheeled around and ran away, fast as I could go.

Only, I didn't go very far. Suddenly, there was

no ground under my feet. I was falling . . . falling . . .

All at once, I was in water. I couldn't breathe. Instantly, my inside feelings took over. My feet paddled and churned, all four working like mad.

My head popped above the surface and I gulped down a deep breath. Frantically, I kept pawing the water. No matter how much I paddled and pawed, I couldn't touch the bottom. I swam back to the side where I'd fallen in, but concrete was too far away. I couldn't reach it. I couldn't get out.

My legs dug the water harder. I turned and paddled to the other side. There was still nothing to grab hold of—still no way out.

I paddled and paddled. My legs were getting tired. I could hardly breathe. Legs churning and sides pumping in and out as I gasped for air, I headed for the other end of the enormous drinking bowl.

It was a long way off, and by the time I got there I was exhausted. My legs felt like they were going to drop off. My head and ears were sinking lower and lower. My nose was barely above the surface.

This was it. This was the end. I was such a happy puppy. I liked my brothers and sisters. I loved my mother. I finally had my My—but now it was all over. I was a goner. And what a way to go—to drown in a drinking bowl . . .

31

Chapter 5

*A*big paw caught me under my chest and belly. The paw lifted me.

I kept paddling.

Even when I was clear out of the water and pawing nothing but air, I kept paddling.

The man People looked at me and shook his head. "Dumb mutt," he sighed. "You're a pointer, not a retriever. You're not supposed to get in the swimming pool."

Dangling in midair, I kept right on paddling until the man People wrapped both paws around me and held me against his chest. My legs were so tired and weak, I could barely move them. Still desperate to get away from all that water, I climbed up his chest and was going clear to the top of his head. I wanted to get as far away from that drinking bowl as I could. But when my front paws draped over his shoulders, he hugged me tight and I couldn't move. I was as high as I was gonna go.

I peeked over his shoulder and looked down. The water in the drinking bowl sloshed and splashed below us as he turned and carried me toward the People house.

"What happened?" I heard my My's voice, but I was so tired I couldn't even turn around and look at her.

"Puppy was sniffin' at a wasp that landed on one of the rosebushes." When the man People talked, I could feel his chest rumble against mine. "Thing stung him on the nose and he ran. Fell smack into the swimming pool. Get some towels."

The man People, the boy People and my My took turns holding me on their laps and rubbing me with these big pieces of cloth. I wasn't really cold, but I couldn't stop shivering. They rubbed and rubbed and rubbed until I was finally dry. I quit shaking.

Then they went inside the People house.

It wasn't long before dark shadows began to stretch across the big yard. I didn't even think about squeezing through the black fence. I sat as close to the People house as I could get. It got darker and darker. I pressed harder against the brick.

Suddenly, light flooded the concrete place where I lay. It went out in kind of a half ring into the big dark yard. I raised my head and looked around. There was a clicking sound behind me. I turned my head and cocked an ear. The door swung open. Cool air rushed out bringing strange smells from inside. People noises came to my ears and perked them up as my My stepped over me.

She reached down and patted my head when I sniffed her leg. "Hello, J.C." Her voice made me feel a little better. My tail wagged just a bit.

I followed her to the edge of the hard gray concrete. She put a bowl down. It smelled good. It was food. Water came to my mouth and my tail whipped back and forth. It was food like back home. Real honest-to-goodness food like my brothers and sisters and I ate. When I bit into it, I found that there was more. There was some sort of red chewy stuff in there with the food. That was REALLY good.

I gobbled it down while my My patted me and watched. She kept talking to me and saying "J.C." over and over again.

The man People came out and sat in one of the People chairs. He scratched a piece of wood on a tiny box and a fire puffed up. He stuck it to a white stick that hung from his mouth, then blew the fire away. Smoke came from the white stick. It smelled nasty.

He puffed on the nasty stick until I was finished with my supper. When he ground the glowing red end of it into a bowl, I went to check it out. There was gray powdery stuff in there and the ends of a whole bunch of those nasty sticks. I could barely use my nose because it had started to swell. I sniffed but only a little air got in. The stuff in the bowl smelled even worse than the smoke. It hurt my nose, then tickled. I sneezed.

The man People petted me and I forgot all about the stinky bowl full of nasty sticks. Beyond the half circle of light where we sat, it was really dark now.

"I'm sure glad you're out here with me." My tail thumped the concrete. "I don't like being alone, especially in the dark. For a while there I thought I was gonna have to sleep by myself. I've never slept by myself before. I don't think I'd like that too much."

The man People made a grunting sound and got up from the chair.

"Hey, wait. Where you going?"

He reached for the door.

I darted in front of him so he couldn't open it. "Hold on just a minute. You're not gonna go inside and leave me, are you? I mean, like, it's really dark out here and there's all sorts of strange sounds and smells and noises and . . ."

He shoved me aside with his leg and closed the door—right smack-dab in my face.

I stood on my hind legs and put my paws on the door. Maybe if he saw me he'd open up and come back out. "Please don't leave me out here all alone. I'm scared. My nose hurts. I've always had someone to sleep beside me. I don't want to sleep all by myself. Oh, please, please, please . . ."

Much to my relief, it wasn't long before the door opened and the People came outside again. They brought the dog with them.

Careful to keep my nose out of reach, I eased over to him. "Hi," I greeted timidly with my happiest smell and wag.

"Chomps, be nice," the man People warned from behind the closed door.

The dog just stuck his nose in the air and ignored me.

The man People blew smoke from one of his nasty sticks. The boy People and my My sat in chairs next to him and made People noises. The dog trotted to the fence and raised his leg. When he was done, he kicked grass at the wet spot with his hind feet.

I walked slowly toward him.

"I'm sorry I'm in your yard," I told him with my eyes and a twitch of my whiskers. "It's not my fault. The People brought me here. Please don't be mad at me. Please don't bite me again."

He sniffed at me. A ridge of hair rose down his back. "Beat it, kid," he growled.

"Chomps!" The man People roared.

Quickly, the dog tucked his tail and backed away. My My opened the door and let Chomps Dog back in the house. As soon as he was gone, I trotted over to the man People.

"You're really nice," I wagged. "You saved me from the big drinking bowl. You told the Chomps Dog not to bite me. Thank you."

I stood on my hind legs and put my front paws in his lap. "Thank you, thank you, thank you!"

He smiled down and patted my head. His touch felt good. I felt safe from the drinking bowl and from Chomps Dog and from the dark that lurked just outside our half circle of light.

"If you'll stay out here with me, I'll be really good. I won't bark or growl or make bad smells. I don't want to be alone. Please?"

He patted me again. I wanted to be closer to him. I pulled with my front paws and kicked with my hind feet. If I could just get up there . . . if I could just get to his lap . . . I pulled harder. I climbed with all my might.

Then his big paw slipped under my rump and he lifted me. The night was scary. My new home was scary. And even though I felt safe in the man People's lap, I still trembled.

"J.C. Puppy's had a pretty rough day." The man People's voice rumbled.

"Sure has," my My agreed. "I never dreamed he could squeeze through the security fence, much less that he'd fall in the pool. If you hadn't come out for a cigarette when you did, the little thing might have drowned."

I felt safe on the man People's lap. Still, a shudder raced through me.

"Think he's a little scared, too," the man People said. "I bet J.C.'s never been alone much. He's always had his brothers and sisters to sleep with."

My My nodded her head. "Sure hate for him to end up in the pool again. And with no one out here to watch him . . ."

The boy People leaned toward her. "Why don't we let him sleep in the house tonight?" he suggested.

The man People and my My both looked at him and smiled. "Bet he'd feel safe and happy if he had somebody to sleep with," my My almost laughed.

Suddenly, the boy People's eyes got really big. "Now, wait. Hold on," he said, waving both arms at them. "I meant in the playroom or the kitchen or . . ."

The man People and my My looked at him and smiled, even bigger than before. The air kind of whooshed out of the boy People's chest.

"Ah, man . . . I can't believe it."

Chapter 6

I couldn't believe it, either. This was GREAT!

Never before had I seen the inside of a People house, much less been in one. But that's just what happened. And even better—I didn't have to sleep all by myself.

The boy was named Justin. I slept with him. We didn't sleep on the cold, hard ground, though. Instead, he tossed me onto this big mat that was far above the floor. At first, I didn't like it. The thing made a sloshing sound when I landed on it. When Justin bounced or flopped around on the mat, it went up and down and made the same sloshing noise that kind of reminded me of the big drinking bowl where I had almost drowned.

For a time, he let me walk around and explore on the big mat. It really felt weird when I walked.

I eased to the edge and looked down at the floor. It was a long ways, so I decided not to jump. He wrestled with me and played with me for a while. That was fun. He laughed when I licked him in the face. He yelled and shoved me around if I bit his big paws or chewed on his arm.

After a while, he got quiet. Then there was a click sound and the light went out. I wanted to play some more. He shoved me down beside him. I tried to crawl up and lick his face. He shoved me down. I tried to go explore. He shoved me down. This time, he held me. One of his big arms wrapped around me from underneath and his paw held my shoulders. His other arm draped over my back and held my bottom. Every time I tried to move, he just hugged me tighter.

The People house was a whole new world. There were a million things to do and places to sniff and explore. But soon, when I finally figured out I couldn't move or go anyplace, I settled down.

It had been a long day. I didn't realize how tired I was until I lay still for a moment or two. My eyes felt heavy. Before I knew it, I was asleep.

The man People came for me early the next morning. My Justin was still asleep and I had just squeezed from under his big paw that was draped across my back. I hadn't even gotten to the edge of the bed when the man People swooped me up in his arms and carried me outside. He put me on the ground, patted my back and said, "Tee-tee, Puppy."

I tried to sniff the grass. That's when I saw my nose. When I looked down my snout, I almost fell over. My poor nose was nearly twice as big as it was supposed to be. It hurt, too. Well, not bad. It only hurt when I tried to take a deep breath or sniff something.

"Tee-tee, Puppy," the man People said again.

He kept saying it over and over. For a while, I thought they must have changed my name while I was asleep. But after I walked around a moment or two and went to the bathroom, he picked me up and patted me.

"Good boy, J.C.! Good puppy! J.C.'s a good, good boy!"

I could tell he was happy. Why, I didn't know, but I liked the way he petted me and the way his mouth noises made me feel.

He plopped his rump in the chair and let me sit in his lap. I liked that, too.

What I didn't like was when he stuck one of those nasty sticks in his face and blew smoke. My nose was so big, I could hardly smell anything with it. I *could* smell that nasty smoke, though. My nose hurt as it was, and the sharp smell from the man People's nasty sticks didn't help.

I got down from his lap and went to explore.

It was a little hard to do. I could always learn more about things and places with my nose. But since my nose hardly worked, I had to use my eyes and ears.

From the trees near the silver barn, I could hear birds chirping. My eyes could see them fluttering and jumping from branch to branch, if I watched really close. I heard the man People go inside the house and shut the door. I saw a grayish brown bird with a long tail and white on its wings land in the tree with the green needles. Then another bird flew into the tree. She had a bug in her mouth.

Suddenly, there was a whole bunch of chirping.

"Me, me!" the chirping said. "That's my bug. You had the last one. Feed me. Me!"

Then the chirping stopped and the birds flew away. In just a moment they were back with more bugs. Then, from a dark spot from inside the tree, the chirping started again.

"Oh boy, two bugs. Mine. Mine. Feed me. Feed me!"

I eased to the edge of the black poles that surrounded the concrete. My head would fit through just fine. So would the rest of me. Still, I remembered the bug with the sharp tail and the big drinking bowl. I hesitated, but for only a second. The birds and all their chirping were just too exciting. I simply had to go see what was going on.

So I slipped between the black bars. I saw the

big drinking bowl. I made a picture of it in my mind so I would be sure not to get too close to it—no matter what happened. Then I concentrated on the tree.

The big birds came back with more bugs. There was more chirping and yelling from inside the tree. When they swooped away I eased closer.

High up in the tree was a bundle of twigs and grass. It was shaped a little like the food bowl my My fed me in last night, only much, much smaller. The chirping came from inside.

Why I didn't rush up to the tree and put my paws on a branch so I could see better, I don't know. There was something inside me—one of those inside feelings that told me to be very quiet. One step at a time, careful not to make a sound, I sneaked up to the tree. Only inches from the base, I stopped.

I heard a fluttering sound. Then a boastful chirp.

"I'm ready. This time I'm gonna do it," the chirp said.

"Well, go," another chirp answered.

"I will. Just give me a second."

"Quit talking about it and do it."

"I will. Just give me time. I'm almost . . . hey, quit. Stop pushin'. Don't . . . Oh, NO! AHHhhh . . ."

All of a sudden, there was a clunking sound from up in the tree. There was fluttering and more clunking and a loud thud. A bird landed right in front of me. Well, he didn't land. He sort of flopped flat on his back. I cocked my head to the side and stared down at him.

I'd never been this close to a bird before. I'd seen them plenty of times, up in the trees or flying to the top of the barn back home. But never, never this close. I tilted my head the other direction and leaned to sniff him. The bird rolled over and got to his feet. He fluttered his wings and kind of shook himself.

"Man, what a trip." He bobbed his head up and down and shook once more. "Hey, Charlie," he called to the tree. "Watch that first step. It's a doozie."

My nose almost touched him. Still, it was so swollen and puffy I couldn't smell anything. I sucked in a deep breath, trying to get a sniff.

Suddenly, his eyes flashed.

"EEeeeee . . ." He screamed. "A monster!"

I snapped my head to the side so I could see it. When I didn't see the monster, I turned the other direction.

"What monster?" I gasped. "Where?"

"Help! Help! The monster's gonna eat me!"

I looked all around, but there just wasn't any monster. So I leaned back toward the little bird and tried to get a better smell.

"You're nuts," I told him. "There's no monster. You and me are the only ones out here."

There was a swishing sound, and out of the corner of my right eye I saw a grayish brown streak. Wings opened and I got a glimpse of white feathers. Before I could even tilt my head to look up at it . . .

WHAM!

Mama bird bit me. Right smack-dab on the tip of my sore nose.

The pain was horrible. It knocked me backward. Head over paws, I tumbled. My tail crunched under me, then my head went *thunk* on the hard ground. It took me a moment to get on my feet. I crossed my eyes and looked down my snout. My nose throbbed and pounded. Water leaked from my eyes.

"You big, bad monster," the mama bird scolded. "You leave my baby alone!"

"I'm not a monster. I'm a bird dog."

She held her wings out so she'd look big and mean. "Go on and get out of here. Leave my baby alone or I'll peck you again."

Crying from the pain, I tucked my tail and ran for the safety of the People house and the man People's lap.

Chapter 7

I learned a whole bunch in the next few weeks. First off, I learned that when your nose gets scratched by a cat *and* bit by a dog, *and* stung by a wasp, **and** pecked by a bird that it swells up really, REALLY big!

For a while, my nose was so huge that I could barely see around it. I couldn't run and play much because I couldn't see where I was going. I was afraid I might run into something. That would make it hurt even more. Mostly I was afraid that I would lose my nose like Old Blue lost his. I made myself a promise that if my nose was okay, I would always take good care of it. I would never, *never* let anything hurt my nose again.

It took a week for the swelling to go down and two weeks before my nose started to work again.

I also learned that my My was named Carol. My Carol fed me and petted me and talked sweet to me. The boy People, called Justin, was my My, too. That's because he loved me. My Justin was full of play and fun. He chased me around the big yard and wrestled with me and laughed when I chased him. I learned that when it was time for bed, if I curled up next to My Justin and lay really still, he wouldn't push me down or clunk me over the head with his pillow.

The man People was named Bill. He was my My as well. He saved me from the enormous drinking bowl, and he talked my Justin into letting me sleep inside at night. When I was scared or hurt, all I had to do was go put my paws on My Bill's leg and he'd lift me up onto his lap and pet me and love me. I didn't like the smoke that came from his nasty sticks, but just being close to him and sitting on his lap was almost enough to make me forget about the stink.

Another thing I figured out was that Gray Cat and Chomps weren't as mean and tough as I first thought.

Gray Cat was a hunter. He caught birds, mice, and rats—mostly rats. He would catch them out by the silver barn. Then he would eat part of them and leave other parts just outside the door to the People house. That was to show My Carol what a great hunter he was. When she woke up in the mornings, she would take me outside.

Sometimes she would look to see if Gray Cat had brought her a present. Other times, she would forget and almost step on the rat parts. Then she would tell Gray Cat what a good mouser he was and pet him. After he went inside, her nose would kind of crinkle up and she'd use a long stick to throw the rat parts way out past the fence. Gray Cat did most of his hunting at night, and during the day all he wanted to do was sleep. I learned that if I didn't startle him or get too close, he wouldn't swat at me with his paw, and he was really pretty nice.

Chomps was a soccer dog. Well, he was really a Scottie, but he was a soccer Scottie. (I guess soccer's big in Scotland.) Anyway, My Justin would come outside every morning with this round black-and-white ball. He'd kick it and chase it around the yard or bounce it up and down on his paw or head or knee. After a while, he would open the black gate with the up-and-down bars and let Chomps come out with him.

My Justin and Chomps played keep-away with the soccer ball. My Justin would kick it with his paw and run round and round the enormous drinking bowl. Chomps would growl at the ball and bite it or try to trap it between his front paws. If he got it, My Justin would put his paw on top of the ball, spin around, and start kicking it in the other direction to keep Chomps from getting it. They laughed and played and ran and ran and ran.

When they were through, they came back in the little yard with the black poles and sat down. They were both panting and out of breath, but Chomps picked up his Wiggie and wanted My Justin to play some more.

Wiggie was a short, fat piece of rope with two knots on either end. Chomps got it in his mouth, growled, and shook it. Then he took it to My Justin and put his paws in My Justin's lap. My Justin ignored him.

"Ah, come on and play," Chomps wagged.

My Justin still ignored him.

"I'll play with you," I said as I trotted up beside them.

"Beat it!" Chomps growled.

I tucked my tail, but before I could back away, My Justin got one end of the rope and began to tug.

"I got it," Chomps growled. "You can't get it away from me. I'm gonna hang onto it forever." Only this growl was different from the growl he used on me. This was a play-growl—teasing and fun.

My Justin pulled and played with him and Wiggie. Then he put one end of Wiggie against the corner of my mouth.

Cautiously, I took it and bit down on the knot.

"Man, you're no match for me," Chomps said

in his play-growl. "I'll drag your tail all over this yard. I'll . . ."

He began to tug and yank. I hung on.

Sure enough, he dragged me all over the yard. We were both about the same size, but Chomps was much older and stronger. Still, it was fun. If I lost my end of Wiggie, Chomps would take off around the yard and I had to chase him. After a while, My Justin opened the gate and let us run and play in the big yard. I was careful not to get too close to the enormous drinking bowl when Chomps and I played tug-of-war with the Wiggie or when I chased him round and round.

I could tell when Chomps was tired of the Wiggie game. The tone of his growl changed. Whenever I heard that, I'd let go of the Wiggie—real quick—to keep from getting my nose bit again.

I learned that as long as I listened and minded him, Chomps was fun to play with. Mostly, he liked to sleep in the sun. But almost every day we played and tugged on the Wiggie and chased and ran. Inside, we played and wrestled on the People bed or on the floor. My Carol and My Justin and My Bill would laugh at us. Sometimes, they even played with us.

I learned that it made my Mys happy if I went to the bathroom, *outside*, when they said "tee-tee Puppy." They were *not* happy if I forgot and

made a mess inside the People house. It also made my Mys happy if I came to them when they whistled and said, "Here, J.C. Puppy." I learned that the enormous drinking bowl was really a swimming pool. My Mys would jump in and splash and paddle from one end to the other. Once, they made me get in it, too. They put me on a pad that floated. My feet got wet and I shook and trembled. But they talked sweet to me and didn't shove me off the pad and into the water. I didn't like the pool much. I think they could tell because they finally let me off the pad. It felt good to have my feet on solid ground.

I learned that potato chips were good. They tasted even better than my puppy food. I learned that the vet was bad. The vet was a big gray building made of blocks. When I went there this lady named Miss Becky pushed and poked me. She looked in my ears and took my temperature. (That was embarrassing.) Then she stabbed me with this sharp, pointed needle that really hurt, and patted me on the head. Going to the vet wasn't fun. When I got home, I learned that snapping at flies *was fun* and that they wouldn't hurt my nose.

Like I said, I learned a whole bunch of stuff. The bestest thing I learned was "go for a walk."

One evening while My Justin was watching TV, I went to lie on the People bed with My Carol. Sometimes, My Justin wasn't ready to go to bed when I was and it was fun to spend time with her. She munched on some potato chips and gave me some. Suddenly, she crunched the sack shut and jumped out of bed.

She stood in front of this bright shiny piece of glass and patted her tummy. Then she used her muscles to pull her tummy in, only when she relaxed, it sort of popped out and she patted it again. She frowned, made a growling sound at the shiny glass, then got foot covers for her paws out of the closet.

The next morning, when I was doing my tee-tee Puppy bit, she frowned down at Chomps. She patted his tummy, then patted her own.

"That's it, Chomps." She made a people noise. "I've had enough of this fat stuff. We're gonna start walking. Ready to go for a walk?"

"Go for a walk" was the best mouth noise People can make. Because "go for a walk" is the funnest thing in the whole entire world.

Chapter 8

I never got to explore outside the big yard where the enormous drinking bowl—I mean pool—was. But "go for a walk" meant that early each morning, My Carol would open the gate and I could go anyplace we wanted.

Well, almost anyplace.

There was a road behind our People house. It was covered with tiny rocks and there was tall grass on either side of it. We walked up a hill, across a long flat place, around a curve, and stopped at a big silver-colored drinking bowl.

"Is that for a big dog?" I asked Chomps.

"Man, puppies sure are dumb." He snorted at me. "That's a drinking bowl for the cows."

"Cows? What are cows?"

"They're these big animals who live behind the People house."

"Do they eat puppies?" I asked, cocking an ear. "Are they mean?"

"They eat grass." He went to sniff at something on the ground. "And they're not mean unless you get too close to their babies. You get too close and they try to stomp on you or butt you with their heads. You leave 'em alone, they're okay."

At the cow drinking bowl, we turned around and walked back to the People house. Then we went back to the drinking bowl. Five times we went back and forth and back and forth.

Each time we walked, I noticed new smells. There were animals who lived in the tall grass. Animals with strange scents that tweaked my nose and made me want to go closer to find out more about them.

Only trouble was, I was too little. If I left the road, the grass was so tall and thick I couldn't get through it or jump over it. Sticks and twigs caught my paws and tripped me. I fell flat on my snout every time I tried to go into that marvelous place to explore.

But by the end of summer, a lot of changes had taken place. First off, we didn't "go for a walk" in the mornings. That was because My Carol and My Justin had to get dressed and go to this place called school. They were gone most of the day and it wasn't much fun not having them around to play with.

My Bill didn't go to the place called school. He went in a little room and punched at keys on a machine. Sometimes, he would let me inside with him. He wouldn't let me climb up in his lap, but I could lie on the floor. As he punched his keys, I could sense his feelings. Sometimes he was happy, sometimes I could feel excitement and adventure. Other times he was sad. All this from doing nothing more than sitting behind his little machine and punching the keys. It was weird.

When My Carol came home after school . . . well, that's when the adventure really started.

Now that summer was almost over, I was bigger and stronger and braver. I didn't have to stay on the road with My Carol and My Bill when we walked. I could leap through the tall grass and go all over the farm where we lived. There were all sorts of smells—cows and skunks, birds and rabbits, places where coyotes had been during the night—the smells were wonderful and exciting. Especially the bird smells. Sometimes, I could hear a rat or mouse scurrying through the grass. When I did, I'd freeze and listen. If I heard him again, I'd go dig around where the sound came from, trying to catch him.

Now and then I'd find something dead. Dead

things smell great. They're like perfume! I'd roll in the dead thing and rub my sides on it so I could get the good smell all over me.

For some strange reason, every time I found dead things to roll in, I got a bath when we went home. I didn't much like baths. My Carol would put me in this big slippery thing with water in it. I didn't like getting wet all over. Then she'd put this stuff on me that bubbled and smelled horrible. Once I got it in my eyes. That hurt something terrible. She'd rub and rub and then wash all the bubbly stuff off.

When she let me out of the water, she and My Justin or My Bill rubbed me all over with towels. Then they sniffed me and made happy mouth noises. I don't know why they were so happy. When they washed the dead-stuff perfume off, I didn't smell very good.

I guess it was worth it to get to sleep on the waterbed, though. I liked my waterbed. I liked being inside the People house. I loved exploring in the tall grass. I was one lucky dog.

Then, one day . . .

My Carol came home from school. My Justin had to go to this thing called soccer practice, so he didn't get home until later. He was always tired and smelled sweaty so he didn't want to "go for a walk" when he came in.

My Carol put her school things away and she and My Bill got dressed to "go for a walk." It took them forever.

I ran to the door, back to the bed, then back to the door again. Finally, they opened the door. Chomps and I shot out and put our paws on the back gate. They opened the gate for us.

Hard as I could, I raced for the tall grass. I was so excited to be out and free, I could hardly stand it. I leaped into the grass and began to sniff. The coyotes had come during the night. Their scent was everywhere. Gray Cat almost caught a rabbit. It was before the coyotes had come, but it was a close call for the rabbit. The scent of fear was still strong.

It was so good to be free. So wonderful to run and chase and smell and explore. This was heaven!

Then it happened.

I needed to check and see where My Carol was. The bottom wire at the place where I came to the fence was so low, I decided to step over it instead of trying to crawl under and scratch my back. I ducked to miss the second wire.

Suddenly, something bit my ear. It was sharp. It hurt. I was running so fast, I couldn't stop. The flesh on the top of my ear ripped. Then whatever bit me pulled me to a dead stop so quickly that my feet flipped clear out from under me. I landed on my side and heard the fence wire go *twang*.

The pain made me yell. I struggled to my feet. Shaking my head, I tried to make the hurt go away. It wouldn't, so I raced for My Carol. She would help the hurt go away. My Carol loved me.

Chapter 9

"**M**ust have caught it on the barbed wire," My Bill said, holding me down.

"Looks horrible." My Carol shuddered and got to her feet. She turned her head. "Does it need stitches?"

"I don't know," he answered. "What do you think?"

"I can't look at it." Her voice sounded sad and scared.

I wiggled, trying to get free. My Bill wouldn't let me go. I shoved with my legs, trying to get up. "It doesn't hurt anymore," I tried to tell him. "It's okay, honest. Besides, I can smell a bird. Come on. Let me up."

He latched on to my ear again and held it out

from my head. It hurt, but I figured if I yelled he'd never let me go.

"I can't tell," he sighed.

My Carol started walking toward the People house. "We better take him to the vet."

My Bill finally let me loose and I took off for the smell that kept tugging at my nose. But before I knew it, I heard the gate open.

My head tilted and my good ear cocked.

They're at the house? What's going on? We just got started. My tail was perfectly still. Both ears were up—away from my head so I could hear. The chain-link gate rattled. My Bill whistled. "J.C. Here, boy!"

What were they doing at the house? I wondered. I better go check this out.

When I got home, Chomps was in the backyard. He trotted around the pool, holding the Wiggie and waiting for someone to play chase with him. When I got to the gate, My Bill opened it for me.

I smiled up and wagged my tail. "What's going on? Why did we come to the house? Chomps in trouble or somethin'? What's the deal?"

As usual, he didn't understand. He just closed the gate behind me, and without a word went into the house.

"What's going on?" I asked Chomps.

"Got me," he shrugged his ears. "Maybe it's time for supper."

"You're always thinking about eating," I let my tail droop. "It's too early for supper."

The door opened and My Carol came out. My tail jerked up again and started to wag because I figured we were going to finish our walk.

Only, before I knew it, she knelt and put a leather strap around my neck. That stopped my tail dead in midswing. I hated the leather strap. When they put that on, the rope always came next. Somebody was always yanking on the darned thing. If I tried to run or go sniff something, I couldn't. It choked me and made me cough.

Next thing I knew, we were in the old bouncy machine monster. My Carol held me next to her with an arm around me. The noisy thing roared and sputtered before we took off. Since the day I came to live with my Mys, I'd almost gotten used to the machine monsters. We'd gone for a number of rides. Sometimes I liked the machine monster. Sometimes I didn't.

Trouble with the machine monster was, I never knew where it was taking us. The last few times I had gotten to go for a ride, we went to a new place. I got to get out and run and sniff and explore while My Bill and My Justin yelled at me and followed me around. That was fun.

But in the back of my mind, I could remember another time when they took me for a ride. That time we went to this big building made of gray blocks. My People called it "the vet."

The vet smelled funny. There were cats and dogs there. I couldn't see them, but I could smell from under the door in the little room. Some were mad and some were scared and some were very, very sick. There were other smells in that room—strange, sharp smells that hurt my nose and made me want to lick myself to get the nasty taste out of my mouth.

Man, I sure hoped we weren't going there.

We stopped at the building with the gray blocks.

I didn't want to go inside. My Carol dragged me. I jerked and jumped, but the leather strap choked me, so I went.

It wasn't as bad as I remembered. This time, Miss Becky just looked at my ear. She didn't take my temperature. I was glad. She only gave My Carol some cream stuff and we got back in the truck.

My Carol put the cream on my ear. It hurt a little when she touched it, but when she was finished it didn't sting or anything. This was great. Now, maybe we could finish our walk.

We didn't walk. Instead, My Justin drove up in his machine monster just about the time we got home. I was the first to get out. I was ready to run and play. I loved My Justin and could hardly wait to get my paws on him.

I hit the end of the rope so hard that I thought the leather strap was going to hang me. No matter how much I wagged my tail and jerked and jumped, My Carol wouldn't let me go. She held on to the rope and we all followed My Justin into the house.

My Bill and My Carol told him about my ear. He looked at it and shook his head. Then he patted me.

"You call Tommy today?" he asked My Bill.

"Yeah," he answered. "Tommy said any time we were ready to bring him it'd be fine."

My Justin folded his arms. "But is he ready?"

"Tommy thinks so," My Bill shrugged. "He's your dog. Yours and Carol's. You two have to decide."

My Justin looked at me a long long time. Finally, he took a deep breath. "Let's do it."

"When," My Bill asked.

"Right now. I don't want to think about it. Let's just take him, now."

My Justin got some sunflower seeds from a package and plopped them in his mouth. My Carol went to the cold box and looked inside for a long time, only she didn't get anything out. My Bill grabbed a nasty stick and went outside.

Nobody was paying any attention to me or petting me, so I went to the bedroom and got the

Wiggie. When I came back, they were all talking again. My Justin lay down on the floor and patted me and loved on me.

It made my tail go thump on the carpet and I couldn't keep my feet still. It felt so good, I forgot all about Wiggie. I licked him and kissed him.

Only instead of laughing and pushing me away, like he usually did, he only loved me more and hugged me tighter. My Bill jingled something in his hand.

"Ready. You two sure about this?"

My Carol and My Justin didn't answer.

A strange smell—a feeling—came to my nose when My Carol knelt down on the floor beside us. She rubbed my head and stroked my back. The smell, the feeling, was scary. Still, I could feel her love inside.

"You be good while you're off at camp." She tried to make her voice sound light, but I could almost feel the tears behind her eyes. "Behave yourself. I don't want you to come home with any bad habits." She rubbed my head and stroked my back. "No smokin' or drinkin' or stuff like that. Understand?"

The sound of her voice made me want to wag my tail, but the sadness and worry that crept through her light tone kept my tail still.

Next thing I knew, we were in My Justin's machine monster. I got to sit in the middle. It was exciting. I watched the birds that flew by and tried to jump and get a better look at them. My Justin kept pushing me down and telling me to sit.

I was a little worried, too. But when we drove right past the building with the big gray blocks, I wasn't worried anymore. Where we were going or what we were going to do, I had no idea.

But like I said, my Mys loved me. They'd never do anything bad to me, so where we were going or what we were going to do . . . well, it really didn't matter.

Chapter 10

Our machine monster roared and rumbled for a long, long time. I got tired of My Justin shoving me down when I tried to look out the windows, so I curled up in the seat and took a nap.

When the machine monster stopped, it woke me up. I sprang to my feet and looked around.

It was a strange place. Out the back of the machine monster, I could see a yellow house. There was no fence around it like at our house. Out My Justin's window, I could see a field. It was big and open—the perfect place for running and exploring and finding new smells. I was so excited, I could hardly wait. I tried to climb over My Justin to get out. He shoved me back. Then I looked out the front.

All of a sudden, my eyes got big. They must

have been as big around as Gray Cat's eyes were the first day he found me in his yard. The air caught in my throat and my tail quivered.

Dogs!

There were dogs everywhere! On my good-ear side, there were rows of small pens with cement floors and wire like around our backyard. On my hurt-ear side, was a huge brown barn. There were pens with dogs in there. Beyond were more rows of dogs. Big dogs. Huge, enormous dogs. Dogs with long hair and dogs with short hair. Some dogs looked like me. I'd never seen so many dogs.

Then My Justin opened the door.

The barking scared me to death. Some barks were happy. Most warned of a machine monster that had driven up. Others threatened—mean and scared and angry.

My Justin got out. My Bill got out.

The barking made me tremble. My Justin pulled on the rope, but I couldn't move. He pulled harder. I dug my toenails into the seat. I didn't want to get out—not here—not in this horrible, scary place.

"Come on, J.C.," he ordered. But when I wouldn't move, he picked me up and set me on the ground. I wanted to go back in the belly of the machine monster. I jumped for it, but he yanked my leather strap and slammed the door in my face before I could make it to safety.

I was terrified. The sounds, the smells . . . it was all so new—so strange and scary.

Suddenly, the barks from all the dogs sounded happy, almost excited. I peeked under the truck to see what was going on.

A man People walked from the house. I could see boots and blue jeans. Clinging close to the safety of My Justin's heels, I followed him behind the truck. The man had hair on his face. Sort of like dog hair, but he was still mostly naked. He touched paws with My Bill and they pumped their arms up and down.

"I do believe that pup's bigger and more developed than the rest of the litter," the man told My Bill. "He's one fine-lookin' pup."

He took the rope from My Justin's paw and began to pull.

"Hold it!" I screamed. "Wait a minute. I don't want to go with you. I want to stay with My Justin."

I locked my arms and dug my paws into the ground. He pulled harder. I fought him. I twisted my head and neck, trying to slip the leather strap over my ears. He dragged me around in front of the truck.

The dogs barked when they saw me. Finally, the man stopped pulling.

"Look at the little punk," a voice barked from one of the pens.

"Ah, he's nothin' but a stinkin' pup," another called.

"If he puts that pup in here, I'll eat him for supper."

"Come on, guys," a girl barked. "He's just a baby. Quit scaring him."

"Looks like supper to me," a deep voice roared.

I felt the hair bristle on my back.

"You can't scare me," I growled, trying to sound brave. "I'll . . . I'm gonna . . . I'll . . ." I stammered, suddenly realizing that I was just too scared even to try and sound brave. "I want to go home!"

All the dogs barked their laughter.

My Justin and My Bill followed as the man dragged me to a row of pens. No matter how much I jumped and jerked or tried to hide behind My Justin, he just kept pulling. I couldn't get away. It was no use.

Before I could even yell "HELP!" he opened one of the pens, slipped the rope off my leather strap, shoved me inside, and closed the gate.

I lunged against the fence.

"Let me out! Please. Don't lock me in here!"

I lunged against the fence again. My Bill and My Justin were right there. They stood looking down at me. "Let me out," I begged. "I want to go home with you. Don't put me in here."

I stuck my nose against the very corner of the tiny pen. There I froze. I didn't move. My tail didn't quiver. I didn't blink. I didn't hardly breathe.

They watched me for a moment.

"Why are you doing this to me?" I wondered. But they didn't hear me—either that or they just didn't understand. "I've been a good boy. I haven't chewed up any shoes lately. And I didn't mean to pee on the floor yesterday. Was it my ear? Is that why you're doing this to me—because I ripped my ear and you don't think I'm pretty anymore?"

My Bill and the man with the fuzzy face went to talk with the dog in the pen next to me. My Justin reached through the fence and rubbed my nose.

"You be a good boy for Tommy," he said. Then he whispered: "I love you."

I stood frozen with my nose pressed into the corner of the cold steel pen.

"It's a lie," I answered without moving so much as a single muscle. "If you loved me, you wouldn't do this to me. What did I do? Why is this happening?"

Then, shoulders slumped and his bottom lip sticking out, he walked away. My Bill left the pen next to mine and paused beside me a moment. "Be a good boy, J.C." he said, trying to smile. He walked away, too.

From the very corner of the pen, I could see them standing behind the machine monster.

They talked for a long time. I couldn't hear their words. There was too much barking and growling all around me.

Maybe they were punishing me for something I had done. My Justin had hit me and talked to me real mean a couple of times. My Carol swatted my bottom and rubbed my nose on the wet spot I left on her carpet. Maybe it was something like that. Soon it would be okay. If they were punishing me, they would come back and get me and hug me and love me—everything would be all right again.

Sure enough . . .

When I saw My Bill come around the truck and walk toward where they left me, I was so happy I thought my tail was going to knock the whole pen down. I jumped up on the fence to greet him. My Bill touched my nose through the fence.

"You be a good boy for Tommy," he whispered. "We love you. You're only gonna be here a couple of months and we'll come back for you."

Then he turned and walked away.

"NO!" I begged. "Please don't leave me!"

He kept walking.

"Come back," I howled. "Don't go away. Please. Don't leave. Please, don't stop loving me!"

I stood for a long, long time with my paws on the fence. I didn't move. I didn't even breathe

deep. The big dogs who lived in the tiny pe
that lined either side of the walk finally qu
threatening me and quieted down. When my hi
legs began to tremble, when My Justin and M
Bill climbed into the machine monster and le
and when I finally realized they weren't comi
back for me, I let go of the fence and stood wi
my nose against the gate.

The lights went off in the yellow People hous
The dogs in the other pens curled up and we
to sleep. All except for one. Someplace, from f
at the other end of the pens, I heard a sound.

Old Blue howled.

It was a mournful sound. Soft and low, it cre
through the darkness of our kennel that cool fa
evening like a snake. The sadness of its cold ha
coils wrapped around me, cutting off the last fa
ing hope that my Mys, whom I trusted and who
I once thought loved me, would ever come bac

I pressed my ears flat against my head, tryi
to shut out his cry. Still it got through. It ma
my insides feel as cold and lonely as he was.
hurt.

Until Old Blue howled, I had no idea wher
was. But when I heard his mournful cry, I
membered Mr. Tommy's kennel and Mother a
my brothers and sisters. I remembered how s
cial My Carol's look made me feel that first d
I saw her and how wonderful her touch was
remembered how excited I was when she put r

in the machine monster and took me to her People house. I remembered how she loved me even when I threw up on the cloth seat of her machine monster. I remembered My Justin and how he let me sleep in his waterbed and how I felt safe and protected. I remembered My Bill who let me lie in his lap and how he talked to me and petted me.

With each memory, the hurt tightened around my heart.

How could my Mys be so cruel? How could they care for me and love me and make me trust them . . . then simply throw me away like an old piece of trash in this horrible and lonely place? How and why would they desert me and break my heart like they did?

I looked up at the half-moon, far away and cold in the black night sky. I took a deep breath. I closed my eyes.

I howled.

It was a mournful sound. Soft and low, it crept from my throat and through the darkness of our kennel that cool fall evening like a snake. The sadness of its cold hard coils wrapped around my heart.

I howled again.

Old Blue howled back.

The sounds were exactly the same.

Chapter 11

"**H**ey, kid. Knock it off!"

The deep growl startled me. My mouth snapped shut and I looked around.

"Huh? What?"

"I said, knock it off! It's hard enough to sleep with Old Blue howling. Now I gotta listen to you, too."

I cocked my ears and leaned forward, staring into the darkness. From the shadows of the pen next to mine, an enormous dog appeared. He strolled over to the fence between our pens.

"Come here, kid. Let me get a sniff so we'll know what's going on."

Cautiously, I moved over to stand near him.

He was HUGE.

I felt my eyes get big and my ears perk up when

he walked over to sniff me. My tail kind of
tucked under me, too. He towered above me and
I stood like a statue when he smelled me.

People animals are kind of weird. When they
meet another People, they don't really know
them. They don't know whether they're nice or
mean. They don't know whether they're going to
hurt them or be friends with them. It takes Peoples forever to truly get to know another People.
Dogs know each other QUICK!
Just a few sniffs, a twitch of the ears, and a
wag of the tail—that's all it takes for us to know
each other. By the time the dog was through
sniffing me, he knew I was named J.C. He knew
I had three Mys, I slept inside on a waterbed, I
didn't like the sharp needles at the vet place, I
was nice, and I didn't want anything to hurt my
nose—not ever again.

"Okay, kid," he said, leaning close to the silver
fence. "Your turn."
I turned and stuck my nose through the little
squares of the chain link to check him out.
Big Mike was a bird dog—just like me.
Well, not really. He was a grown-up bird dog.
He had a long, pointy tail, just like me. He had
a good nose, just like me. He was mostly white
with brown spots on his ears and side. His brown
spots were dark and mine were more lemon

color—but still, his markings were kind of . . . just like me.

From his smells, he had told me that he once had a My, but the People wasn't happy with him, so he sent him back to Mr. Tommy's kennel. Big Mike loved to hunt birds called quail. He was big and tall and strong and he knew about everything there was to know.

Then he told me the very best thing of all.

"Mr. Tommy's training me so I'll be a better bird dog. Pretty soon, I think your Mr. Bill will come back and take both of us home."

All four feet gave a little hop, all at once. When he said that, I spun to face him.

"He'll come back?" I panted. "He'll take both of us home?"

Big Mike shrugged an ear. "Yep. At least I think so."

I pushed my nose clear through the chain link until it stuck and I couldn't get it to go any farther. "You mean they *didn't* desert me? They won't leave me here forever? I won't have to howl at night like Old Blue? You mean, they'll come back for me?"

"Of course, you dope." He wagged. "Couldn't you smell how much they love you when they told you good-bye? They hadn't even left and they already missed you and wanted you back home."

My tail stuck straight in the air and I jerked my nose out of the fence.

"Are you sure?"

"Sure, I'm sure!" He wagged. "You got it made, pup. I mean, any bird dog who gets to live inside a People house, sleep on a waterbed, and get to take baths in the People bath bowl—man, you got it made for sure. I bet even if you never pointed a bird in your life, they'd still love you."

"Would they be proud of me?"

He flipped his tail to the side and sat down.

"Well, that's another matter," he answered with a shrug of his ears. "Your My is proud of you when you point quail. That's about it. But that's what you're here for—to learn. Now shut up and get some sleep. We both got a lot of learning to do tomorrow."

With that, he turned and went inside the big barrel in the middle of his pen. I didn't like the barrel in my pen. It smelled of Fat Mary, the dog who had lived here last. She wasn't a happy dog. She loved to eat, but when she did she got so fat she could barely run. They didn't feed her as much as she wanted, so mostly she was mad and unhappy. The barrel smelled of that, so I slept on the cold, hard concrete floor of my pen.

I *made* myself go to sleep! Even with the scary noises that came from the other pens—even on the cold, hard ground instead of my waterbed and even with Old Blue's howls that sent the chills up my spine—I made myself sleep. That's because the next day, I would start learning to be a bird dog. I would work hard. I would do everything that Mr. Tommy wanted me to. I would be the world's greatest bird dog and my Mys would be so proud of me!

I worked hard. I learned all there was to learn. I didn't yank on the rope too hard and flip myself over when we went to the field. When Mr. Tommy or Roberto would throw the squishy thing with the feathers in it and yell "Fetch," I would chase after it and bring it back to them. I didn't bite it too hard, and when they said "Give," I opened my mouth and let them have it. I didn't run back to the pen when Mr. Tommy made the loud BOOM with his big double-barrel boom-boom stick. (A dog called Sam did that all the time. It made Mr. Tommy very, VERY unhappy.)

And when I found a quail . . . they were easy to find because they had the most wonderfully delicious smell that ever came to my nose . . . anyway, when I found them, I would follow them real carefully, so they wouldn't fly away. When they stopped, I stopped. Then I pointed at them, just like a good bird dog is supposed to do.

The moon came full two times. The nights became cool and crisp and the days not so hot and long. And just like Big Mike had promised, my Mys finally came for us. I could hardly wait to show them how much I had learned. I could hardly wait to feel what Proud was.

When I saw my Mys, when I smelled them, my tail wagged so much that it shook me all over. It shook me so hard that even my ears flopped.

"I really am sorry," Mr. Tommy told them. "That's the risk you run when you buy a puppy instead of a fully grown dog who has already been trained."

My Bill looked down at me and sighed.

"Are you sure?"

"Afraid so." Mr. Tommy sighed back at him. "He's broke to the rope and collar. He's not gunshy. He stops when I give the command. He knows how to fetch and give. He doesn't bust coveys or singles. It's just . . . well . . . I guess his nose doesn't work. He won't point birds."

"What do you mean, my nose doesn't work," I gasped. "My nose works great. I really protect it, too. What are you telling them?"

"Not even once?" My Justin asked.

"Not even once," Mr. Tommy answered. "A couple of times, he acted like he was on a point. I mean, he freezes—gets really still. Only, his head's down between his front paws and his ears are dangling on the ground. When I kick around

84

n front of him there's not a bird. Darndest thing
I've ever seen. I could work with him longer, but
I'm afraid it would just be a waste of your money.
I really am sorry. I'll tell you what, though. If
you want a dog who's already trained, I'll give
you the money back you spent on training J.C.
and see if I can find him a good home."

"Why are you lying to them like this?" My tail
drooped and slipped between my hind legs. "I'm
a great pointer. I point quail all the time. Why
are you telling my Mys this?"

My Bill was not proud.

My Justin was sad.

My Carol was happy to see me. She loved me
very much. But no scent of Proud came when
she reached into my pen and scratched behind
my ears.

For an instant everything was quiet. No birds
chirped in the trees. No dogs barked. Through
the stillness, no sound came to my ears. A sound
came to my heart, though. The sound of Old
Blue's cry.

Chapter 12

I got to go home. I got to live in the People
house. I got to sleep in the waterbed with My
Justin. I got to sit in My Bill's lap in the evening
when he blew smoke from his nasty sticks. He
petted me and loved me. My Carol gave me baths
in the People bath bowl and loved me just like
I'd never been gone. They all loved me, but they
weren't proud.

Big Mike got to live in a pen behind the silver
barn. Almost every day, when My Carol and My
Justin came home from school, my Mys would
go hunting. They put on bright orange caps and
bright orange vests. They picked up their boom-
boom sticks, got Big Mike out of his pen—but
they left Chomps and me home.

I snapped at flies or slept in the sun. Sometimes, I could hear the bang from their boom-boom sticks in the fields. When I did, I would jump up on the gate and beg for them to let me go with them. Just once I wanted to show them what a great pointer I was.

When they came home, I could smell the quail. It was a deliciously wonderful smell. I could smell Proud when they would pet Big Mike and give him an extra helping of food before they put him in his pen.

More than anything in the world, I wanted to feel proud.

Snow came. Little sparkly, silver crystals fell from the sky. The nights got really cold. The snow went away but the nights and days stayed chilly.

My Carol didn't like the cold. She was a little afraid of the boom-boom sticks, too. I could smell it on her. Although her boom-boom stick wasn't as big as the ones My Justin and My Bill carried, she just didn't like them all that much. So she began to stay home with Chomps and me.

I would lie beside her on the People bed while she put little red marks on papers. The papers came from the place she called school. Each one had a special smell of a different People. Most People papers smelled good. One smelled mean and sneaky. A couple of times I smelled where one People copied the very same thing another

People had written. My Carol must have smelled it, too. It made her really mad and she made a big red X on the whole People paper.

When it was almost dark, My Bill and My Justin would come home. Sometimes they smelled happy and proud. They smelled of quail. Other times, I didn't smell the quail on them. I didn't smell much Happy or Proud, either.

I stayed in the People house and longed to hunt quail and to feel proud.

Then one day it finally happened.

My Bill and Justin took Big Mike and left in the machine monster. My Carol put her school stuff on the bed and took her school clothes off. With nothing to do, I plopped on the People bed to wait for her. Sometimes she patted me while she was making marks on her People papers. Chomps jumped on the bed and lay down beside me.

"You want to play?" I asked.

He just flopped over on his back and closed his eyes.

My Carol looked down at him and frowned. Then she stood in front of the shiny piece of glass. She patted her tummy and frowned even more.

"That's it!" She snapped. "Cold or not, I've got to get some exercise. Wouldn't hurt you either, Chomps. You guys want to go for a walk?"

The familiar words "go for a walk" perked my ears and made my tail drum on the bed. When I saw her putting on her "go for a walk" shoes, I jumped from the bed so fast I almost broke my neck.

I ran to the door and put my paws on it. I ran back and jumped on the bed. She was still getting dressed. I ran back to the door, back to the bed, and back to the door. It took forever before she was ready.

When she opened the gate, I raced ahead of My Carol and Chomps. Gray Cat had caught a rat near some trees by the road. It was a big rat and had put up a pretty good fight. No coyotes had been around in a week or two. The rabbit who lived under the brush pile had seen me coming and was hiding.

I stood on my hind legs and looked around. My Carol was already headed up the hill. I raced to get ahead of her, because good bird dogs are always supposed to hunt in front of their My. I caught her and raced ahead to check out the plum thicket where the road turned.

That's when I smelled the wonderfully delicious smell of . . .

Quail.

I froze. The scent locked my legs and my head and my tail—every single muscle in my body tensed.

89

I tested the air again. They were close. There was more than one. More than two. There were a whole bunch of them. Without moving so much as a whisker, my eyes darted about. I saw them.

The quail stood together in a circle in the center of the plum thicket. Their tail feathers touched in the center of the circle and they watched, outward, so they could fly away to escape. Too close to risk getting any nearer to them, I pointed. I held them. As long as I didn't move, they didn't fly or run away.

I heard the footsteps. My Carol and Chomps came closer and closer.

But they didn't stop. They kept going.

"No! Come back. Quail!"

My Carol kept walking. Farther and farther down the road. Suddenly, she stopped.

"Come on, J.C." she called. "Come on, boy."

I didn't move. I didn't even twitch.

"They're right here. I'm pointing at them. Please . . . please see them."

My Carol came back. "Chomps, what in the world is that stupid pup doing?"

Closer. Closer.

Only she went the wrong direction. I could hear her stomping around in the brush, kicking at the grass. But she was going the wrong way.

"No," I said. "Right here. Right where I'm pointing. Why can't you see them?"

"Come on, J.C." she ordered. "This is ridiculous. I need to finish my walk."

My Carol started to leave.

"Wait, I see them," Chomps barked. Then quick as a flash, he charged past me on his short little stubby legs. I didn't even have time to yell at him to stop.

He raced smack-dab for the quail, yapping and barking every step of the way.

They flew. There was a sound of their short wings drumming the air. Feathers knocked against limbs of the plum thicket as they fluttered and scattered in every direction. Chomps barked louder.

And above the sound of the flying quail and Chomps barking, I heard My Carol.

"Well, I'll be darned."

She didn't let me go after the quail. Instead, she kept calling and yelling at me. Reluctantly, I followed her back to the house.

I waited in the backyard. She put Chomps in the house. When she came out she had on her orange cap and her orange vest. My Carol didn't like the boom-boom stick. The thing kind of scared her. But she brought it with her—that's how much she loved me.

Chapter 13

It was after dark when My Justin, My Bill and Big Mike came home. I played tug-of-war with Chomps and Wiggie. As far as I was concerned, Chomps was my best friend. If he wanted to play, I would play. If he wanted to sleep, I would leave him alone. If he wanted to eat his food *and mine* both—that was great. Anything he wanted was fine, because without him My Carol might have never seen the birds in the first place. There was no way I could ever thank him enough.

My Bill and My Justin didn't smell of quail when they came in. They didn't smell of Happy, either. They put their boom-boom sticks in the box and locked the door, then came into the kitchen.

My Carol hugged My Bill.

"You boys have any luck?"

My Bill sighed and shook his head.

"Nope. Didn't see one single bird all afternoon." He sniffed at the thing on the stove. "What's for supper?"

My Justin came to the kitchen, too. I let Chomps have Wiggie, and I followed him.

"Smells good," he told My Carol. "What is it?"

My Carol smiled. Even from behind My Justin, I could feel the proud.

"Quail."

My Justin jerked. My Bill's eyes got sort of big around.

"Quail?" they both said at the same time.

My Carol nodded her head. Her Proud feeling was even stronger. My Bill folded his arms and stared at her. My Justin lifted the lid off the thing on the stove, just to be sure. Then they both tilted their heads to the side.

"How . . . when . . . where . . . ?" they both sputtered and stammered.

My Carol stuck a stick with a flat silver end on it into the hot thing. It sizzled when she turned the quail over. I could smell the deliciously sweet aroma. She acted busy with her cooking and pretended to ignore them.

"Somebody bring us some quail?" My Bill asked.

"No. I shot them."

My Justin and My Bill frowned at each other.

"Who went with you?" My Justin asked.

"Just me and J.C."

The Proud that came from her made my chest fill and my tail wag.

My Bill's mouth flopped open. My Justin's eyes crossed and he shook his head.

"No way!"

My Carol shrugged and put the lid back on the hot thing.

"J.C. pointed them and I shot them. It's as simple as that."

Gasps and questions and other mouth noises filled the kitchen. They were so loud and so close together it almost hurt my ears. My Carol wouldn't answer them.

"I can't tell you, I'll have to *show* you," was the only thing she said.

That night my Mys ate quail for supper. My Carol gave me two to eat, all by myself.

My Justin got up before the sun the next morning. I wanted to sleep, but since I didn't like sleeping alone, I followed him into the back room. He turned on the noise box with the pictures. While he watched cartoons, I slept on the couch.

I guess he wanted to go hunting. He kept pushing the button on the noise box until it was so loud I couldn't sleep. My Bill and My Carol finally got out of bed and came in with us. My Bill looked disgusted at him when he turned the noise box down, but I could tell he really wasn't.

My Mys put on their orange hats and orange vests. They unlocked the box and got their boom-boom sticks out. Then all of us went hunting.

I don't think I was ever so happy in my whole life. Finally . . . finally, I got to take my Mys hunting.

Back and forth, I raced in front of them as we walked. We were clear on the far corner of our farm before I found the quail. It was a different covey from the one My Carol and I played with yesterday. There were a lot of birds in this bunch.

I found where they had spent the night. I could hardly tell which way they went. I sniffed and worked and sniffed. Yes. This way. They stopped here to eat. The smell was stronger now. They got a drink here in the pond.

"This way," I told my Mys. "Follow me, they went this way."

The scent was much stronger now. Strong and wonderfully delicious and . . .

Then I saw them. They scurried through the tall grass in front of me. I froze, then followed them, one step at a time. Creeping, easing closer and closer and closer until suddenly they stopped.

Beneath the limb of a cedar tree, they gathered with their tail feathers touching in the center of their circle. They faced out, ready to fly away if

I came any nearer. I stopped and pointed them for my Mys.

"What's he doing?" My Justin asked.

"He's on point," My Carol answered.

"A point?" My Justin's voice made a gulping sound when he swallowed. "It looks like he's getting ready to do a somersault."

"Yeah," My Bill agreed. "He's got his front legs apart. The top of his head's almost touching the ground between them. If he put his head down another inch or so and leaned forward, he'd roll right over. What's he doing, pointing with his ears?"

"No, his tail!"

"His tail?" My Justin and My Bill gasped together. "Any bird dog I've ever seen points with his nose."

"J.C.'s not *any* bird dog. He's special," My Carol said. "Where the tip of his tail is pointing—that's where the birds are."

The Proud that came from My Carol almost made my tail wag. But if it did, I might scare the quail. I stood frozen, watching the birds between my legs and pointing at them with my tail until my Mys walked toward the cedar tree and scared them up.

The boom-boom sticks made their loud noises. One quail fell and the others flew away. Most landed in the tall grass down in a valley. Five more flew back near the pond. As soon as I knew

where they went, I raced to pick up the quail that fell when their sticks said *bang.*

I brought the bird back and gave it to My Carol, then I told them to follow me. I showed them where the singles were and pointed them for my Mys.

We had quail for supper that night.

"Darndest thing I ever saw in my life," My Bill said when he finished eating. "Bird dogs point with their nose—not their tail. I just can't figure it out."

My Justin agreed with him.

"I've got an idea," My Carol began. "I think it happened when he was a puppy."

"What happened?" My Bill asked.

"Well, remember when we first got him?"

"Yeah."

"Remember how Gray scratched him and Chomps bit him and then he got stung by the wasp and ended up in the pool?"

"Don't forget the bird who pecked me," I told her, only she didn't understand.

"His nose puffed up like a balloon," My Justin added.

My Carol nodded. "Well, the way I figure it, everything on the whole place went for that poor puppy's nose. My guess is that he decided he was gonna get that nose ripped clear off him if he didn't protect it. So when he finds quail, he tucks his head between his front paws and under his body so nothing can get at it. Then he points with his tail."

"You finally figured it out," I said with a wag of my tail. "Peoples are kind of slow, but you *finally* got it."

"That's the craziest thing I ever heard," My Bill scoffed. Then he looked at me and smiled. "But why he points with his tail instead of his nose . . . well, it doesn't matter. He's one heck of a bird dog."

My Bill sat on the couch and patted his legs. I wagged my tail again and hopped onto his lap. I was getting pretty big—almost grown—so my head draped over his lap on one side and my rear end draped over on the other.

My Justin and My Carol came to sit with us. With my head in her lap, My Carol scratched behind my ears and loved my face. My Justin sat close and put my rear end on his lap. He patted my rump and scratched the good place, right where the base of my tail starts. My Bill rubbed my tummy and patted my middle.

The aroma of the quail we had for supper lingered in the air. It was a wonderfully delicious smell. But Mother was right. It was only the *second best* smell there was. The Proud that came from my Mys was by far the *best!*

I knew that Big Mike and my Mys and I would go on lots of quail hunts. I knew that I would always love my Mys and that they would always love me—no matter what. And I knew that never again would I make that horrible sound that crawls through the night like a snake. Never again would I hear myself cry the sound of Old Blue's howl.

About the Author

BILL WALLACE has had a number of dogs in his life, but none has "wormed" its way into his heart as quickly as J.C. A pointer pup, J.C. was born on April Fool's Day. While searching for a trained bird dog at a kennel in Oklahoma City, Bill and his son Justin (not to mention the dog trainer) were "shocked" when Bill's wife Carol spotted the puppy and decided they should take him home.

Excited and frightened, the puppy threw up in the car on the drive back to the family farm in Chickasha. Gray Cat scratched his nose, Chomps growled and snapped at him, and when the coyotes howled that night, J.C. crawled into Bill's lap and shivered.

J.C. now sleeps on the bed, swims in the pool, chases birds in the backyard, and "points" with his nose. He also curls up at Bill's feet and helps the author while he works on his books.

Bill Wallace's novels have won seventeen state awards and made the master lists in thirty states.